Boys
on Safari

By
Roger Priddy

Gabe, Wallace the dog and Teddy are best friends.

Gabe's favourite book is about giraffes.

He wanted to go and find one in the park.

The three explorers packed for their journey.

They got to the park and began their search.

Wallace saw
a squirrel,
and
chased it.

"Naughty dog!"

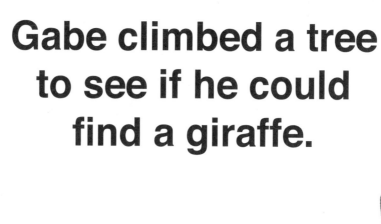

Gabe climbed a tree to see if he could find a giraffe.

No giraffe, but he did find a bird on a nest.

And Wallace
found a
butterfly.

From the tree they could see a duck pond.

But where were the giraffes?

The three friends rowed across the pond.

A dragonfly flew past.

And fish swam in the water below.

They saw a duck looking for her ducklings.

Suddenly there was a big splash!

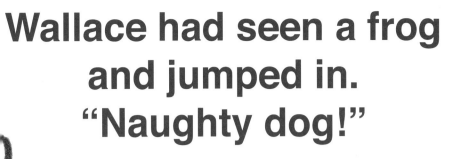

Wallace had seen a frog and jumped in. "Naughty dog!"

Wallace dried off and the friends had their picnic.

From the bushes they heard a noise:

"Quack, quack!"

They looked through the long grass.

Was it a giraffe?

No! They had found the lost ducklings.

Wallace carefully carried them back to the pond.

The ducklings were back with their mummy.

"Quack, quack!"

Gabe was sad not to find any giraffes, but happy to have returned the ducklings.

The three friends went
home. It had been
a long day.

They went to bed
and dreamt of more
adventures.